ISBN: 0-7172-8907-9

Grolier Books is a Division of Grolier Enterprises, Inc.
Manufactured in the United States of America.
A B C D   1 2 3 4

GROLIER
BOOKS
BOOK CLUB EDITION

One morning, deep in the
African jungle, a gorilla named
Kala was walking toward the
feeding grounds. Kala had just
lost her baby. She felt sad and
all alone. Then suddenly…

"Waaah!"

She heard a noise. A baby
noise! Kala followed it to a tree house.

"Waaah!"

The crying came from inside.
Curious, Kala entered.

There she found a human baby. Kala had
never seen one before. It looked funny.
Kala sniffed. It smelled funny. It didn't even
have fur! But it was sad and all alone.

Kala gently picked the baby boy up. He stopped crying. She cradled him in her arms, and he smiled. Kala's heart filled with love.

ROAR!

It was Sabor the leopard! Kala clutched the helpless babe and ran out.

She had to escape! But how? Kala saw a boat
attached to a rope. Desperate, she jumped in.

Whump! The
boat fell safely to
the ground below.
Sabor tried to
follow but got
tangled in the cord.

Kala brought the baby to her family.

"It's freaky-looking!" laughed a young gorilla named Terk, "but it's kind of cute!"

But Kerchak did not agree. Kerchak was Kala's mate and leader of the gorillas.

"Take him back," Kerchak said flatly. "He's not one of us. He could place us all in danger."

Kala refused. The baby needed her,
and she needed him.
"You will be my son," she said to
the smiling child, "and your name
will be Tarzan."

Five years passed. Tarzan grew strong and active.
A little too active!

Sometimes his high spirits got him into trouble.

One day Tarzan got into serious trouble.
He accidentally caused an elephant stampede.
Kerchak was furious!

"You almost hurt someone!" Kerchak scolded.

"He's only a child," Kala defended him.
"He will learn."

"He will never
learn to be one of
us!" Kerchak
replied angrily.

Kerchak's words hurt Tarzan.

"Why am I different?" Tarzan asked sadly.

"You're not different," Kala replied. She put Tarzan's hand to his heart, and his ear to her chest. Tarzan felt their hearts beat together.

"See?" Kala said, smiling. "Exactly the same. Kerchak just can't see that."

"I'll make him!" Tarzan cried. "I'll be the best ape ever!"

Years went by. Tarzan became a strong, young
adult. One day he was wrestling with Terk.

"Okay! Okay! You win!" Terk cried. "Let go!"

The friends were having fun. They heard a ROAR!

It was Sabor! The leopard chased them back
to the feeding grounds.

Kerchak fought to protect his family but was
badly wounded.

Tarzan leaped to the rescue! He defeated Sabor with his trusty spear. Then the ape man let out a mighty victory cry!

"AH-EE-AH-EE-AH!"

Tarzan had saved the family.

Tarzan placed Sabor's body at Kerchak's feet. He bowed in respect.

BANG!

A loud noise thundered through the jungle.
The apes ran off. But Tarzan was curious and
went toward the sound. He found something
amazing. Creatures just like him.

"Clayton, don't shoot!" Jane scolded. "My
father and I are here to see gorillas. You'll
scare them."

"Gorillas are wild beasts," Clayton replied coldly.

Tarzan could not take his eyes off them, especially Jane. He watched as she sketched a young baboon.

"My, you are a sweet little one," Jane said.

The baboon stole her sketch book then ripped out pages!

"Hey, you little art thief!" Jane cried. "Give me that!"

Jane angrily yanked the drawing back. The young baboon started crying. Suddenly, Jane was surrounded! It was the baboon's family. And they were angry!

Tarzan swung into action! He carried Jane to safety.

"Oh, my goodness!" she cried. "I'm flying!"

Tarzan and Jane talked but spoke different languages.

"Tarzan!" he said, pointing to himself. He was telling her his name.

"Oh, I see!" she answered.

"Oh-I-see," Tarzan repeated, pointing to Jane.

"No, no, no. I'm Jane," she corrected.

"No-no-no-Jane," Tarzan replied, still pointing.

Eventually, they worked it out and became friends.

Tarzan took Jane back to her campsite. What
a mess! While the humans were out exploring, the
apes were having fun.

"Hey, Tarzan!" Terk cried. "Look what we found!"
Jane could not believe her eyes.

"Gorillas!" she gasped. "And he's one of them!"

Kerchak arrived. He saw Jane. To him, she was a stranger, a danger to the family. He pounded his chest to scare her.

"Oh, my!" Jane screamed in terror. Kerchak ordered the family to leave. Sadly, Tarzan followed them, leaving his new friend behind.

"Protect the family," Kerchak ordered Tarzan. "Stay away from the strangers!"

But Tarzan couldn't. He had to see Jane again. He returned to the human camp. There, he met Clayton and Jane's father, Professor Porter.

Jane decided to become Tarzan's teacher.

The days passed. Jane showed Tarzan books, music, and science. Tarzan learned to speak English and thrilled to the wonders of Jane's world.

And Tarzan shared his world with Jane.
He took her up into the trees. Jane saw the birds,
the animals, and the vast beauty of the wild.
She felt close to the jungle and even closer
to the jungle man.

Then something terrible happened. Tarzan learned that his human friends would soon leave, and never come back.

"Not come back?" Tarzan asked sadly.

"If only we saw some gorillas," Clayton said. "That is why we came."

Tarzan did not want Jane to leave. Ever.
So he led the humans to the ape nesting area.
The gorillas were afraid but soon relaxed.
Some baby apes danced for Jane.
"Nice to meet you!" she said, laughing.

Professor Porter also made friends with the apes.
"Hello! Archimedes Q. Porter at your service,"
he said. "Uh, quite a grip you've got there."
Even Clayton was pleased.
"My dream has come true," he said slyly.

Suddenly Kerchak arrived! Clayton reached for his gun. Kerchak moved toward the humans.

"No!" Tarzan shouted. He leaped on Kerchak and held him tightly as the humans escaped.

"You betrayed our family," Kerchak growled at Tarzan. "I knew you'd never be one of us."

Tarzan felt awful. He had actually defied Kerchak!
"I'm so confused," he sighed to Kala.

"Come with me," Kala said. "There's something
you must see."

Kala took Tarzan to the tree house where she
had found him as a baby. There, Tarzan saw pictures
of his human family.

Tarzan decided that his real home was with
humans. Tarzan dressed in his father's clothes
and hugged Kala good-bye.
  "You will always be my mother," he told her.
  "And you will always be in my heart," she replied.

The next morning, Jane and the others prepared to leave.

"Oh, Tarzan!" Jane cried, seeing him. "I'm so glad you're coming!"

"Yes," Professor Porter added. "Jane would not let us leave without you."

As they boarded the ship, Tarzan took one last look at his home.

But it was a trap! Once on board, Tarzan, Jane and
Professor Porter were captured by Clayton and his
men. Clayton tied them up.

"Why?" Tarzan asked in shock.

"For money!" the evil hunter replied.

Clayton planned to capture the gorillas and sell them.

"I couldn't have done it without you," he laughed.

Tarzan cried out in despair.

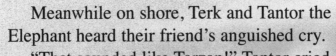

Meanwhile on shore, Terk and Tantor the Elephant heard their friend's anguished cry.

"That sounded like Tarzan!" Tantor cried. "He's in trouble!"

Tantor and Terk raced to help their friend.

Back on board the ship, Tarzan and the others
were locked up below deck when...
CRASH!
Terk and Tantor burst through the ship's hull!
"Thanks, guys!" Tarzan shouted.

Tarzan ran to the hole in the ship.
"Where are you going?" Jane asked.
"To save my family!" Tarzan replied.
Then he dived into the water and
swam for shore.

Clayton and his thugs were at the nesting area.
One by one, they rounded up the gorillas. Clayton
spotted Kerchak and reached for his gun.

"I think this one will be better off stuffed!"
he sneered.

"AH-EE-AH-EE-AH!"
Tarzan arrived to free the apes.
"You came back," Kerchak said.
"No. I came home," Tarzan replied.

Just as Jane was freeing Kala…
BANG!
Clayton fired at Tarzan! Kerchak bravely rushed to
protect Tarzan.
BANG!
Kerchak was shot by Clayton.

Clayton chased Tarzan high into the trees.
There they fought. Tarzan took the rifle.
   "Go ahead. Shoot me," Clayton teased.
"Be a man."
   Tarzan smashed the gun.
   "Not a man like you," he answered.
   Clayton got tangled in the vines, and
he fell to the ground far below.

Meanwhile, Kerchak was fading fast.
Tarzan held the great ape in his arms.
"Forgive me," Tarzan said.
"No, forgive me," Kerchak gasped.
"You have always been one of us.
Take care of our family, my son…"

The next morning Jane and Professor Porter prepared to leave for England.

"Good-bye, Jane," Tarzan said sadly. "I will miss you."

As the boat pulled away, Jane gazed longingly at Tarzan.

"Jane, I think you should stay," Professor Porter said. "Go on. You love him."

Jane knew he was right. She jumped out of the boat and into Tarzan's arms.

Professor Porter also stayed. He was happy to spend his life studying gorillas. Jane was happy to be with the man she loved.

Tarzan was the happiest of all. He found his
true home and family. Here in the jungle, he and
Jane would live very happily ever after.